At The Home Of The Winter King

AMY LAURENS

OTHER WORKS

SANCTUARY SERIES

Where Shadows Rise
Through Roads Between
When Worlds Collide

KADITEOS SERIES

How Not To Acquire A Castle
Define Good

STORM FOXES SERIES

A Fox of Storms and Starlight

SHORTER WORKS

Darkness and Good
Dreaming Of Forests
Of Sea Foam and Blood
Trust Issues

NON-FICTION

How To Write Dogs
How To Theme
How To Create Cultures
How To Create Life
How To Map
The 32 Worst Mistakes People Make About Dogs

Find other works by the author at
www.amylaurens.com

At The Home Of The

Winter King

INKLET #35

AMY LAURENS

www.inkprintpress.com

Print ISBN: 978-1-925825-34-3
eBook ISBN: 978-1-925825-34-3

www.inkprintpress.com

National Library of Australia Cataloguing-in-Publication Data
Laurens, Amy 1985 –
At The Home Of The Winter King
44 p.
ISBN: 978-1-925825-34-3
Inkprint Press, Canberra, Australia
1. Fiction—Fantasy—Contemporary 2. Fiction—Fantasy—Dark Fantasy 3. Fiction—Short Stories

First Print Edition: June 2020
Cover image © Cyan Art via Deposit Photos
Cover design © Inkprint Press
Interior art © Amy Laurens

AT THE HOME OF
THE WINTER KING

IMAGINE, IF YOU WILL, A YOUNG BOY—
about seven, say—who thinks he's the
cleverest thing in the whole damn
world. Sadly for him, he's not far
wrong—but clever doesn't also mean
wise.

This kid, this boy—this genius—has
played in the bush behind the house
forever, and he knows every gum tree,
knows the curve of white eucalypt
limbs, the smell of leaves baking in the
sun, the feel of a sneeze coming when

the wattle-puff pollen dances in the aid. He knows the needle-sharp sedge grass and the tiny, smiling faces of the billy buttons, miniature suns waving in the breeze; he knows the smell of the snow wind as it rushes off the mountains in the winter, and the taste of the crystal-bright water from the stream, all iced mineral and sweetness.

He wanders through the bush at his leisure, sometimes wandering all the way down to the edges of the pine plantation lining the highway that's the artery of this little two-bit town called Jilamatang. Regional Victoria, back of the Snowy Mountains, over an hour to the nearest thing they've got to a city: he's outgrown the place and he isn't even in double digits. Good thing they have the internet, even though the connection's slower than the post from Melbourne.

He scouts far and wide, spends the whole day exploring while his parents think he's a good lad in school—an easy ruse because school's also easy—and one day, he discovers something worthwhile. Not far from town, a couple of kilometres or so, there's an old train line, rusted iron, smells almost like blood. Barely anyone remembers it, and even the real old timers hardly know it's there.

But *he* knows.

It's always been a demarkation, the eastern border of his domain, and he's had in mind that he probably oughtn't cross it. Crossing it, he feels, is maybe a step too far from his parents' world.

But of course, one day, his curiosity gets the better of him and, breath held by tightly pressed lips that quiver with anticipation, he skips across old rails rusted to the colour of fox's fur.

At first, nothing seems to have changed. The air tastes the same, of warm eucalyptus and baking bark, the same wind blows against his skin with the smell of pine needles, and the same sun beats down upon his shoulders like comfort, like healing, like love.

Then the trees grow denser, gnarled eucalypts and tufty wattles giving way to lofty, straight-trunked pines, needles flared against the bright sun and crisp air of early autumn. *Their* leaves will not succumb to the on-coming cold.

Never mind that neither will the eucalypts'; the pines would have everyone know that needles, at this altitude, this close to the highest mountain in the whole damn country, are superior—which is why *their* trunks are so tall and straight, while the poor little natives twist and bend, backs crooked in submission to the wind.

The thick mat of rust-coloured needles devours the boy's footsteps more effectively than any carpet, and for a while it's eerily quiet, only the slightly sweet, musty smell of decay for company. It grows colder, too, and the boy shivers, even though summer still lingers in the air in long, hot afternoons, and the true bite of winter is still months away.

Through the dense boughs of the pines, something shifts, and he catches glimpse of something moving, something big—something alive. And although his heart pounds like it wants to escape his chest and run right back home to the safety of his kitchen, although the taste in the back of his throat is dust and anxiety, the boy continues.

This, he knows, will be a sight worth seeing.

He follows the half-glimpsed beast for maybe thirty minutes, though of course it seems that either seconds or hours have passed, and then—at last—he reaches a clearing in the pines where granite boulders pile up high, like someone has torn away the skin of the world and exposed its spine, mats of rust-coloured needles like drying blood, the smell of stone and minerals rich in the air and on his tongue.

And there, atop the boulders, head thrown high against the sky, antlers broad and strong enough to tear apart the fat, grey-bellied clouds, stands the last thing he'd have expected to find in alpine Australia: a giant, grey deer, easily as tall at the shoulder as the boy himself—and he is hardly short for his age.

The stag tosses its great antlers, and the boy can feel—*feel*—the words the stag would say, if it could talk—if it *would* talk.

Welcome, the stag says. *Welcome to the home of the Winter King.*

The boy bows politely, because it seems like that is a thing that should be done, and when he straightens up again, the stag is gone.

But he knows, now, the boy, where

this Winter King lives, and now he'll never leave it alone.

Time after time he returns, at any hour of the day: the crisp, bright light of a dew-covered morning, the frosty bite of a late autumn evening, the blazing hot midday summer sun as he runs through the bush, wild and free while school is out.

Time after time, the boy returns to the Winter King, and slowly, he begins to love him. Both hims, that is, come to love the other him, and they stand with each other for hours, foreheads pressed together or flank to flank, surrounded by the smell of deer musk and little-boy sweat, saying all the things the Winter King would say if the Winter King ever decided he wanted to speak.

The boy rubs the knot at the end of the Winter King's spine, right before it turns into a tail, and brings him sweet carrots and apples and old-fashioned lumps of cane sugar. The Winter King whispers secrets into the little boy's heart, right before it turns into his consciousness, and feeds him joys and delights too subtle for words to make out. Probably, the Winter King enjoys it as much as the boy does, for although the boy is lonely—at school, at home—at least he has his parents, and they love him very much.

The Winter King has no one.

Well, that is not quite true, the boy learns. The Winter King has his storm foxes, ethereal spirits that ride the winds like hawks, soaring and diving and tumbling. The storm foxes love the spring storms best of all, when thunder splits the sky like canons and the lightning flashes strobe-like across the forest and the smell of ozone is thick in the air.

The foxes love the storms because storms bring freedom: the Winter King cannot contain them when the heavens open and rage, and through spring and especially summer, his power wanes almost completely.

But then, one day, the boy has no one either. His mother and father fought, and although that wasn't unusual, the fact that his mother left and didn't come back was.

He didn't realise until later what the little plastic stick in the bathroom bin three weeks ago had meant; why his mother had cried for three full days before the fight that ended it all; why his father had been so relieved to see her go.

Not that he ever said he was relieved, and the boy knew his father missed his mother—but he also walked as though a great weight had been lifted from his shoulders. An important weight.

A weight of about seven or eight pounds, if the boy understood things correctly, that would last some eight or nine months and then for the rest of their lives.

The boy thought he might have quite enjoyed that weight. It might have been just heavy enough to keep his family together.

But alack, the weight had vanished—from his father's shoulders, his mother's body—and so his mother vanished from their family, and the boy felt all alone.

That was the night it happened. The night he told the Winter King what he wanted—and the night he learned that sometimes, what we want is the worst thing we can imagine.

He was supposed to fly. He'd been talking about it with the Winter King for weeks, toying with the idea the way one might flirt with a bit of dandelion fluff: a present and passing delight, nothing serious, nothing weighty.

And then his mother had left, and his father might as well have: for all his father's relief, he remained cold, remote, and distant for the boy. Might as well take up residence with the moon.

And so, he'd been talking to the Winter King for weeks about what it might be like to be a storm fox, about how the Winter King had made them for company in the first place, and now—*now*—the dandelion clock had landed, the seeds begun to take root, and the Winter King discovered that even ethereal fluff is terribly tenacious once it's grown a taproot.

Possibly, he was not as surprised by this as he made out to be, for his efforts at dissuading the boy were tokenistic at best, and the boy was determined: if the Winter King could not send his foxes out to find his mother, then he, the boy, would go instead, and since he could not drive, and could never follow her on foot, they would do what they had been inadvertently planning for weeks, and the Winter King would turn him into one of the foxes, and he would find his mother that way.

The Winter King wondered, momentarily, if this was what the boy really wanted.

But the boy, lungs full of almost-winter chill, nostrils thick with the sharp, sweet, acrid scent of wood-smoke, heart heavy with the weight of long, cold nights alone, knew what he wanted, and what he wanted was this: to make his father sorry.

The distant foxy yips made the hair on the back of the boy's neck stand on end. For a moment, he rubbed his arms and wondered whether this was what he really wanted.

But he knew what he wanted, and what he wanted to was to make his father sorry, and so he stood there, soundless, still, in the shadow of the boulders in the dying of the evening light as storm fox spirits swooped from the darkness of the trees and surrounded him. He stayed silent as they nipped at him, experimentally at first, then harder, meaner, surer.

The boulders weren't the only thing that smelled of iron in the clearing.

Tiny wounds, so tiny, barely scratches, but they stung like nettle burns and blood dripped freely, as though it has forgotten how to clot, as though it was crying all the tears the boy had wanted to release but found somehow instead wedged tightly in his throat.

His pulse raced, and the blood ran freer, and underneath the stinging burn, his skin began to itch. His vision hazed, blurring into red for a moment before returning, sharper than before.

The smell of fox musk grew.

So did his fur.

And then, abruptly, the Winter King's foxes all withdrew, vanishing into the pines with eerie yips and cries, and the boy sank to the ground at last.

The tree seemed taller—until he realised that actually, he was shorter.

He flared his canine nostrils, and a fierce joy sang through him at the plethora of scents: pine needles and granite boulders and decaying needles absolutely, but also the musty smell of black cockatoo feathers, the sweet decay of a possum somewhere out there under the trees, the savoury, mushroomy flavours of the fungi on the fallen logs, the rich, thick loam of the dirt way down underneath.

He threw his nose to the sky and laughed, an eerie cry like a cloud covering the moon. *Now* he would find his mother, no matter what the cost. He leapt.

He was supposed to fly.

Instead, the ground knocked the wind from his lungs like disappointment—and he learned that even foxes, real, solid, ground-bound foxes, can cry, if they're truly sad enough.

THE MAKING OF *AT THE HOME OF THE WINTER KING*

I think this is about the fourth iteration of this particular story. It started in the Australian spring of 2014, when I was browsing my sister's Tumblr. It was full of gorgeous, atmospheric images of cable-knit sweaters and rain boots and hands holding each other and foggy pine forests, and something about it just grabbed me by the heartstrings and wouldn't let go.

That initial impression collided with some beautiful images I'd seen on DeviantArt of fox spirits soaring through the air, and became the *Storm Foxes* series.

At The Home Of The Winter King is an integral piece of backstory that also conveniently stands alone as a separate story. It's gone through, as I said, about four different iterations as I refined the magic system of the world and the interactions between the characters and their voices and so forth, but in early 2019, when I was working on editing the first novel in the series, the story finally clarified itself, and here we are.

If you love it, consider checking out the novels, starting with *A Fox Of Storms And Starlight*—you can read the first chapter just over the page ☺

DOWNLOAD YOUR FREE EBOOK

When you buy a print book from Inkprint Press, we like to say THANK YOU by offering you the ebook for free!

Please head to www.inkprintpress.com/inklets/35/ and the use the coupon 35INKLET to get your copy of this Inklet in epub AND mobi today!
(Coupon will only work once.)

Read more by Amy Laurens!

A FOX OF STORMS AND STARLIGHT

CHAPTER ONE

SIX YEARS AGO, I SAVED a fox in the bush. It was only because my dog died. At the time, it felt like a pretty crappy bargain.

It was the first day of autumn—not by the calendar, but by the fresh bite in the morning air, the golden quality of the light as it lit the main road through town in the mid-afternoon.

Sailor was a big, black shaggy thing, something like a Newfoundland, a lively shadow in the golden light, and I was eleven.

I'm sorry to be starting any story this way, but the fact of the matter is, this where it all began.

I'll spare you the awful details. Enough to say that Sailor had got out of the yard somehow, and had been hit by a smallish truck careening down the highway that split our tiny town in two as it blatantly ignored the speed limit.

I saw it happen.

And although I cradled him in my lap as the smell of burnt-out brakes and hot asphalt and turning leaves filled my nose, his giant, furry black head all of him I could hold, there was nothing I could do.

There was nothing anyone could do.

I knew that, but it didn't stop the knot of frustration and guilt in my chest, or the taste of bile in the back of my throat every time I closed my eyes and saw the truck hitting him, again and again and again.

It took years for that vision to fade.

But that evening, only a few hours after it had happened, everything still felt fresh, and raw.

Sunny, my sister, was only nine at the time. She cried for hours, just sobbing like she'd never breathe right again.

I'd cried a little, at the scene with Sailor's head lying in my lap as his big, brown eye stared up at nothing.

It had been mercifully fast, there was that.

And the driver had copped a massive fine—speeding, reckless driving, I think they even defected his truck—and came to visit us later, a big, pot-bellied man standing on our front verandah, shuffling his royal blue cap round and round and round in his hands as he apologised.

But that evening, with Sunny sobbing her heart out on the couch in the living room and Mum and Dad trying desperately to console her as dinner burned on the stove, I couldn't cry, even though the acrid scent of burning soy sauce, scorching brown sugar and smoking rice wine from the marinade prickled the back of my throat and the corners of my eyes.

I was the eldest, and I had to be responsible.

Possibly, if I'd been just a little more responsible, Sailor wouldn't have died.

So I slipped out the glass slider from the family room to the deck while Sunny cried, glancing up at the two storeys of our moody grey house behind me before jumping down the three steps from the rail-less deck to the lawn, and set out for the gate in the back fence.

I couldn't cry, and I didn't want to add anything to an already chaotic and stressful situation inside—but I couldn't stay there, either.

In the gaps between the gum trees to the west, the sky tinged to red and gold at the horizon, the sun sinking slowly into oblivion. I'm pretty sure I didn't know the word oblivion back then, but I knew what it meant, how it felt—and I craved it, desperately.

Anything would be better than the gaping hole in my chest.

And so, because I didn't know where to find it or how to get there, I stalked through the bush, pushing myself until I breathed hard and my lungs ached and sweat ringed me, chasing the way that hard exercise elevated me over my constantly looping thoughts.

Directly above, dark, heavy clouds obscured the sky, and the air was thick, heavy, humid.

Beneath the smell of dry gum leaves and even drier dirt, I could catch a hint of ozone, and occasionally the wind turned cool for a breath as it gusted against my skin, promising a late evening storm.

I strode harder, faster, outpacing the video looping in my mind of the truck's impact.

When the first drops of rain spat at me from out of the sky, I barely noticed. My skin was filmed with sweat, slick and salty, and the peppering of rainwater barely added to it.

That was at first.

But within minutes, it became clear that those first pattering spits had been the early foreshadowing of a storm darker and more intense than any I remembered.

Thunder rolled across the sky, distant and grumbling at first, a lazy background chorus to the rhythmic melody of the rain as it splattered down on grey-green leaves and red-tinged twigs, turning the silvered bark of an old, dead gum to deep grey and making the spiky, tussocky grass seem oddly luminescent in the dying light.

I stood under a grey gum with stains down its trunk that the rain was turning orange, arms wrapped around myself, shivering hard—and for the briefest instant, thought about not going home.

Mum and Dad would pitch a fit.

And I had to be responsible.

I turned, dark t-shirt plastered to my skin, dark hair sticking to my face and clinging to my neck, and began trudging my way back.

The storm closed over properly, clouds rolling over the horizon and cutting off the thin scythe of blood-coloured sunset, making the bush dark and unwelcoming in the premature night.

Lightning flashed.

Thunder cracked hot on its heels.

I jumped—and stared hard at the gap between two ghost-barked trees, where for a second, I was sure I'd seen a pair of eyes.

Nothing moved.

Nothing except the drenching rain, anyway, weighing down the branches that tossed fitfully in the wind.

My pulse slowly calmed.

The rumours we'd all grown up with, indoctrinated since both, spoke of something strange and dark... but in the forest north of here, in the pines, the plantation—not here, not in the natural, native bush.

I shivered.

The smell of wet dirt and soaked bark rose around me, undercut by eucalypt and ozone.

If anything had the power to wash away the hurt inside me, this storm was it. I tipped my face to the sky, imagining that the rain washing over me had the ability to wash me inside as well, and the raindrops splattered hard on my cheekbones, my chin, my tightly closed eyelids.

More lightning. More thunder, cracking over the constant hiss of the falling rain.

And in the distance, something eerie, lifting the hairs on the back of my neck: a strange kind of high-pitched howl, a cry that rang with moonlight and distance, cutting straight through the noise of the storm.

Bolts of lightning streaked across the sky—one—two—three—in the space of half a second, followed immediately by a growling crack of thunder so immense it vibrated in my chest.

I ducked down instinctively into a crouch.

There, in the corner of my eye…

I froze, crouched with my arms over my head.

The strange cries came again—and they were closer.

I stared hard at the place, low to the ground, where I was sure I'd seen something small, maybe the size of a cat.

Flash. Growl.

Rain spitting down.

There. Right there. A small animal, pointy ears, light coloured chin and throat…

The strange, eerie cries came a third time, and my heart pounded fiercely. Whatever was making the noise, it was close. Really close.

The little creature across from me reacted too, flattening itself to the ground.

My jaw twitched.

My heart pounded.

My fingertips bit into my upper arms.

Stay? Go?

Run? Freeze?

The hairs on my neck prickled again and goosebumps broke out all over me.

Cold dread formed a knot in my stomach.

Something was coming.

Something worse than the storm.

I had to get home.

I made it halfway to standing—and a series of strange, awful noises made me freeze again. They were sharp, clacking, squealing sounds, like someone knocking two echoing stones against each other, interspersed with high-pitched yowling…

The creature in the darkness screamed.

I threw my back against the gumtree behind me, pressing hard against it.

My heart hammered.

I peered back and forth in the dark, eyes wide.

Rain drenched down, but my throat was dry.

My pulse pounded faster.

The little creature screamed again—and as lightning flashed, I saw it on its back, legs slashing wildly as something attacked.

The awful, clicking-yowling noises sounded right in front of me.

I slapped my hands over my ears, gasping. Water ran down my face, getting into my mouth, my eyes.

It was hurting.

Whatever the small thing was, it was getting hurt, and I'd seen enough animals hurting today.

Something in my chest snapped.

I flung myself across the ground, leaping a couple of tussocks and a fallen branch before I crashed to my knees.

I crawled closer, desperate, gasping for air through the heavy curtains of rain.

I couldn't see it. Where?

Somewhere here, near the base of that tree…

The yowling screeched right next to my ear. I cowered against the ground, spiky grass pricking my face, wet-earth smell smothering me—but now, there was a strange mustiness too, a cousin to wet-dog smell.

At the next flash of lightning, I saw it.

The creature was a fox—and something barely visible was attacking it, only the gleam of eye or flicker of teeth visible in the gloom.

But the damage was real enough.

The little fox's side had been opened right up, and in the bright, stark flashes of heavenly electricity, the blood was dark, thinned by the constant rain.

No. No more animals were going to die today.

Not when this time, I could do something about it.

I snatched at a branch on the ground that turned out to be more of a glorified twig, and launched myself toward the creature.

I had no idea what was attacking it, but I screamed and waved my handful of twiggy leaves anyway, batting them in the air over the fox like I knew what I was doing.

The horrible clacking cries ceased abruptly.

With one long, low rumble, the rain began to ebb.

I poised, waiting.

But nothing came.

The attackers were gone.

Still gasping for air, pulse galloping in my throat, I sat next to the fox and shifted it carefully into my lap, realising as I tasted salt that I was crying.

I huddled over, trying to shelter the poor creature from the slackening rain, running my fingers over its wiry cheek—over and over and over and over.

"Please," I sobbed, throat tight and aching, chest constricted. "Please. Please don't die. Please."

Please, I prayed to anything that might be listening. *No more death. Not today.*

Not today.

Another gust of cool air washed over the clearing, taking the last of the rain with it—and lifting the goose-bumps on my arms again.

And as it did, I could have sworn I heard a voice. *Neither do I wish him to die now.*

I shivered, drawing the fox close, like it was a stuffed animal I could hug for comfort—its comfort or mine, I couldn't say. I glanced around the dripping bush, eyes wide. The rumours spoke of an evil presence, and I could easily believe that might be what had attacked the fox.

But a voice? No one had ever mentioned a voice.

There was nothing to be seen, and anyway the voice had sounded kindly—and didn't want the fox to die.

Assuming I hadn't just imagined it, of course. Which, half-drowned by grief, the other half drowned by the storm... An over-active imagination seemed highly likely.

Can you fix him? I thought it hard, though, just in case someone really was listening.

Something shifted in my lap.

Around us, the world stilled, dazed from the storm, but also something more, something watching, something waiting, as the bush held its collective breath.

The only sound was the occasional drip of rainwater from the gum leaves onto a fallen log—no insects, no wind, no rustling of leaves.

Just... stillness.

And the fox, who shivered in my lap.

The clouds tore open, revealing a ragged triangle of stars that glittered in the fox's eye as it blinked open and stared up at me.

My chest snagged.

My throat ached from crying, and a headache was forming in the back of my head.

But the fox blinked up at me—alive.

I ran a finger down it again, from nose to cheek to ear to shoulder, all the way down its side to its thick, bushy tail—and the wound in its side began to close.

Laboriously, it hauled itself to its front legs.

I tried to stop it—"No, it's okay, you can stay here, I'll look after you"—but it lifted its top lip to show half-hearted teeth, and staggered away.

As it did, I thought perhaps its fur began to shrink.

And suddenly, it looked larger in the night—as large as a dog, as large as Sailor…

But I blinked, and it was just a trick of the light, because the creature that darted away into the bushes like nothing was wrong at all was clearly a fox, the size of a large cat or maybe a small beagle, and nothing more.

And if something screamed in the night not long afterward, and the cry sounded horribly, horribly human?

Well.

I was halfway back toward home again by then, and I pressed my fingertips to my lower eyelids and prayed my parents wouldn't murder me for getting home so late.

Keep reading! Head to
http://www.amylaurens.com/
books/storm-foxes/
to buy your copy now!

ABOUT THE AUTHOR

AMY LAURENS is an award-winning Australian author of fantasy fiction for all ages. She loves mixing magic with the Australian bush. Further examples of this are the portal-fantasy *Sanctuary* series about Edge, a 13-year-old girl forced to move to a small country town because of witness protection (the first book is *Where Shadows Rise*) and the young adult *Storm Foxes* series about magic and mental health.

Amy has also written the humorous fantasy *Kaditeos* series, following newly graduated Evil Overlord Mercury as she attempts to acquire a castle, and a whole host of non-fiction.

Find out more at:
www.amylaurens.com

Welcome to Dark Dale
LIANA BROOKS

When War Came to Town
A Powers Story
AMY LAURENS

Not Fantasy
AMY LAURENS

Courting the Winter Prince
LIANA BROOKS

At the Home of the Winter King
A Storm Powers Story
AMY LAURENS

With This Ring
AMY LAURENS

Venus &
Seven Reasons I Said No
LIANA BROOKS

OATH KEEPER
AMY LAURENS

FORGET
A Powers Story
AMY LAURENS

INKLET #040
NOT QUITE
Cinderella
LIANA BROOKS

INKLET #041
ONE BAD MAN
AMY LAURENS

DOUBLE ISSUE
INKLET #042
The Claustrophobia
Of Loneliness &
Adam, Be A Star
AMY LAURENS

INKLET #043
The
Artist
as a Young Girl
LIANA BROOKS

INKLET #044
CONFESSIONS
AMY LAURENS

INKLET #045
But For Snow
A Kadhesos Story
AMY LAURENS

INKLET #046
The Boy
Named NO
LIANA BROOKS

INKLET #047
Anamata
AMY LAURENS

INKLET #048
A Wolf FOR
Christmas
AMY LAURENS